ROGER HARGREAVES

mr. men book of silly rhymes

A Thurman Book
PRICE/STERN/SLOAN
Publishers, Ltd., London

To Sheila Snow
for all her help

First published in 1985 by Thurman Publishing,
a division of Price/Stern/Sloan Publishers, Ltd,
PO Box 45, Bromley, BR2 6ES

Phototypeset by Kalligraphics Ltd
Printed in Great Britain by
Maurice Payne Litho Ltd

My name is Mr Silly!
And welcome to my book!
So, let us step inside it now
And take a little look!

I live in a place called Nonsenseland,
Which nobody can understand!
Where the dogs wear hats!
The pigs go, "Moo!"
The trees are red, and the grass is blue!

He's here! He's there!
Beware! Beware!
Mr Tickle is everywhere!

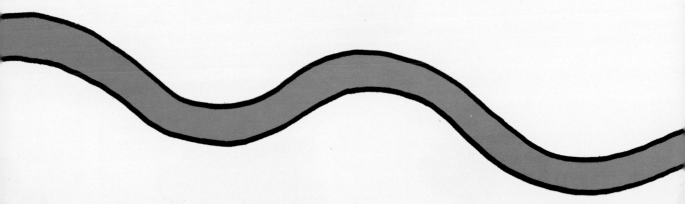

He tickled a frog!
He tickled a dog!
He tickled a fish in the lake!
He tickled a bee!
He tickled a flea!
He tickled a slithery snake!
He tickled a cat!
He tickled a rat!
He tickled a duck and a drake!
He tickled a goose!
He tickled a moose!
He tickled a tortoise awake!
He tickled a snail!
He tickled a whale!
He tickled a crocodile's mate!

And the frog and the dog and the fish
in the lake, and the bee and the flea
and the slithery snake, and the cat
and the rat and the duck and the
drake, and the goose and the moose
and the tortoise awake, and the snail
and the whale and the crocodile's
mate,
They all cried, "That's not nice!"

But he said, "What's the harm?"
As he reached out an arm
And began to tickle them twice!

When Mr Funny stood upside down,

He found his smile became a frown!

Mr Topsy-Turvy
He talks like that!

It's the same way up
As he wears his hat!

Mr Small, or so it seems,
Fell into a jar of jellybeans!
His only means of escape was to eat
The jellybeans!
Which took all week!

Mr Worry, as you might have guessed,
Is down in the dumps. He's feeling depressed!
But there's really nothing that you can do,
When Mr Worry is feeling blue!

Exactly whose odd pair of shoes
Made Mr Mean to stare?
The shoes belonged to Mr Strong!
But what a funny pair!

Upon his right, one shoe was white!
The other one was black!
"I've never seen," said Mr Mean,
"A pair of shoes like that!"

Strong looked at him, and gave a grin!
And said that he knew where!
"Come home with me," he said, with glee,
"To see the other pair!"

Mr Greedy lives to eat!
Mr Greedy likes his meat!
Potatoes, too, by the score.
And when he's done, he asks for more!
Mr Greedy's quite a size.
Mr Greedy loves French fries!
Mr Greedy's tooth is sweeter.
Mr Greedy!
What an eater!
Ice cream sundaes!
Mondays, too!

On candy bars, he likes to chew!
Baked beans on toast,
And in between,
Plates and plates of rich ice cream!
Fish and chips, with sauce on top.
Mr Greedy cannot stop.
Mr Greedy!
Quite a figure!
Day by day he's getting bigger!
But, all in all, one mustn't grumble.
Except about his tummy rumble!

Mr Clever had a performing flea!
He trained it to stand on its head!
He even trained it how to speak!
And, decided to call it Fred!
But!
Along came Mr Silly!
With his hat upon his head.
But he couldn't see!
So he trod on the flea!
And that was the end
of Fred!

Mr Nosey poked his nose
Into a hive of bees!
So, off to Mr Bump he went,
And said, "Oh, please! Oh, please!
A bandage may I borrow,
To stop me feeling ill?"
So that is what he lent him!

And then sent him the bill!

Underneath his nose it grows!
But, wouldn't it be weird,
If, as well as his moustache,

Old Fussy grew a beard?

There once was a worm with a wiggle,
That made Mr Uppity giggle!
His hat fell off! Which made a Toff
Of that upper-class worm with a wiggle!

Into a hole fell Mr Bump!
He landed with a mighty thump!
Mr Silly to the rescue came!
But fell in too!
Oh, what a shame!
He also landed with a thump!
On top of Bump!
The silly chump!

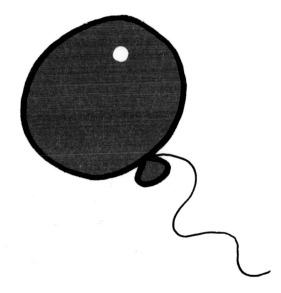

Mr Muddle thinks that black is white!
Mr Muddle thinks his balloon's a kite!
His balloon is here,
But where is he?
The page you're reading
Is twenty-two!
But!
Mr Muddle's on thirty-three!

One baked bean on a plate!
That's everything Mr Small eats!
And a can of baked beans,
When eaten like that,
Can last for fifty two weeks!

Oh, dear! Oh, dear!
What's this I hear?
Mr Noisy's playing the drums!
But, what is worse,
Much worse, I fear!
Is, while he drums,
He **hums!**

Mr Silly to Scotland went!
And guess what he did see?
He saw a sheep!
The sheep said, "Baa!"
And then jumped over a tree!

Mr Silly, he laughed and laughed!
And then he looked at me!
"It's a Scottish woolly jumper!"
Said he, to me, with glee!

Mr Greedy went to Paris.
He travelled in disguise.
Why did he go?
A holiday?
No!
He went to buy French fries!

Mr Happy's round and fat!
Mr Happy's more than that!
Mr Happy's round and yellow!

A round and yellow happy fellow!

Mr Funny sat on a worm!
Which the worm didn't think was funny.
"Gerroff!" said the worm.
"Go, sit somewhere else!"
So!

He went and sat
on a bunny!

They say that Mr Chatterbox talks
The hind leg off a donkey!
But, if he did that,
That Chatterbox chap,
Would make the donkey wonky!

Mr Strong blew up a balloon!
No balloon could ever be finer!
But, it burst with a
"POP!"

And was heard by a lot
Of people living in China!

Mr Muddle fell into a puddle
And got extremely wet!
He caught a cold, and went to get
Cough mixture from the vet!

Roll up! Roll up! It's come to town!
The Mr Silly Band!
Just come and listen to it folks!
The worst band in the land!

An elephant plays the trumpet!
The harpist is a squid!
An ostrich plays the tuba!
On piano is a pig!

An octopus is the drummer!
On banjo is a snail!
A chimp is on the cello!
And the singer is a whale!

A centipede does a tap dance!
On flute a unicorn!
A monkey plays the bongos!
And the rhino plays his horn!

Roll up! Roll up! It's come to town!
The Mr Silly Band!
And, guess what he has called it?
It's called The Elastic Band!

Mr Lazy cannot sleep!
So Mr Lazy's counting sheep!
Ninety-three!
And ninety-four!
Ninety-five!
And ninety . . .

SNORE!

Mr Uppity, in his top hat!
Very rich, and extremely fat!

Two Rolls-Royces, and of course a yacht!
He always winters where it's hot!

All his furniture is antique!
He drinks champagne, seven days a week.

He's a millionaire, or, so it's said.
But his favourite meal is jam and bread!

Mr Impossible flapped his arms
And found that he could fly!
So he flapped and flapped, and flapped and flew
Right up into the sky!

He landed on the moon with ease!
And guess what he did find!
He found the moon was made of cheese!
And he'd landed on the rind!

The world is very large!
And I am very small!
I admit to being little!
As I'm not tall, at all!

But, when I look around,
I'm glad that I'm not tall!
You see, I think, I think that the
Best things in life are small!

The winkle is better than the great white whale!
A breeze is better than a howling gale!
The raindrop is better than the ocean deep!
And a molehill is better than a mountain peak!

The worm is better than the slithery snake!
A shiver is better than a great earthquake!
The poem is better than the alphabet!
And a tom-tit is better than a jumbo jet!

The mouse is better than the mighty moose!
A gosling is better than a big, fat goose!
The dewdrop is better than the River Nile!
And an inch is better than an uphill mile!

So, here is what I think!
That when they all suggest
That biggest always means the best!
I think I must protest!

Mr Bounce went to Wimbledon.
But what he didn't deserve,
Was, while he was there,
He was thrown in the air,

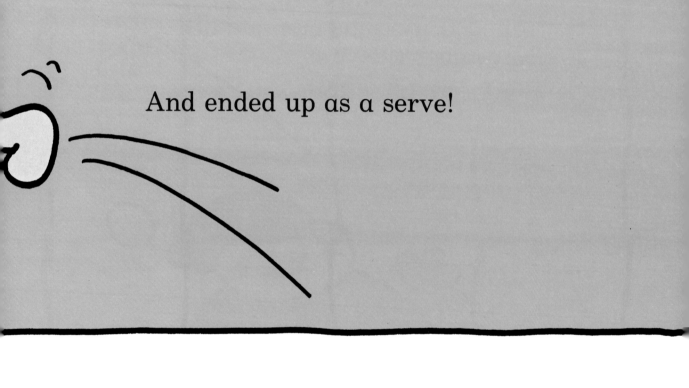

And ended up as a serve!

Mr Forgetful can never remember
That Christmas day is in December!
So Happy Christmas one and all!
It's November the first,
And he's having a ball!

Oh, me!
Oh, my!
Oh, well I never!
If you can read this page
You're Mr Clever!

Mr Worry worries,
While Mr Lazy snores!
Mr Busy hurries!
And Mr Chatterbox bores!

Mr Uppity's rich!
And Mr Strong has strength!
Mr Small's a titch,
And Mr Tall has length!

Mr Grumpy's always cross!
Mr Quiet he never talks!
Mr Forgetful's at a loss!
And see how Mr Funny walks!

Mr Noisy's very loud!
Mr Fussy's rather fickle!
Mr Daydream is a cloud!
Watch out for Mr Tickle!

Mr Bump has had a fall!
Mr Silly's very funny!
Mr Clever knows it all!
And Mr Dizzy is a dummy!

Mr Nosey knows what's what!
Mr Slow is always late!
But, of all the jolly lot of them, . . .

Mr Greedy takes the cake!